This book belongs to

_____

Walt Disney ®

VOLUME 4

GOOFY'S BIG RACE

WALT DISNEY FUN-TO-READ LIBRARY

A BANTAM BOOK
TORONTO • NEW YORK • LONDON • SYDNEY • AUCKLAND

Goofy's Big Race   A Bantam Book/January 1986   All rights reserved.   Copyright © 1986 Walt Disney Productions.   This book may not be reproduced, in whole or in part, by mimeograph or any other means.

ISBN 0-553-05577-1

Published simultaneously in the United States and Canada.   Bantam Books are published by Bantam Books, Inc.   Its trademark, consisting of the words "Bantam Books" and the portrayal of a rooster, is Registered in U.S. Patent and Trademark Office and in other countries.   Marca Registrada.   Bantam Books, Inc., 666 Fifth Avenue, New York, New York 10103.   Printed in the United States of America   0 9 8 7 6 5 4 3 2 1

Goofy had a car, a good old car. It had many bumps and dents. But he loved it a lot. "Bessie takes me where I want to go." He patted his old car. "Nothing stops this car."

Just then Donald drove by. "You call that
a car?" laughed Donald. "That car is just a
pile of junk! Look at the way _my_ car's roof
can go up and down."

"Well, Bessie's roof would go up and down, too, if she had one," said Goofy. "But the important thing is that Bessie always comes through."

"Hah!" said Donald. "Let's see which car is better. We'll race to the ice-cream shop in Horner's Corners."

"Okay," said Goofy. "See you there!"

"Last one to Horner's Corners is a slowpoke!" Donald called.
He drove away fast. *Va-ROOOM!*

Goofy blew his horn. *Ah-OOOO-gah!*
"Come on, Bessie," he said. "Slow and
steady, steady and slow. That's the
way we always go." And away he drove.
Chug-a-chug-chug.

Donald looked at his car. "I want my car to look its best when I win this race. I think I will get it washed. A minute won't matter," he thought.

Donald found a car wash. He drove inside.

He pushed a button to make the car's
roof go up. It would not. He pulled the roof.
He pushed the roof. He kicked the roof. "Go
up!" he yelled. But the roof would not go up.

With a *whoosh*, the water poured over
the car. Out came the car, shiny and clean.
Out came Donald, angry and wet.

"I am soaking wet!" he yelled. "And so is
the inside of my car."

He stopped at his house to dry himself.
He wanted to dry the car seat, too. "A minute
won't matter. Goofy is nowhere in sight."

Goofy chugged along in his dented old
car. "Slow and steady, steady and slow, that's
the way to go. And it always seems to work."

People waved at Goofy. He waved back.
He blew his horn just for fun. *Ah-OOOO-gah!*

Finally Donald was nice and dry. So was the car. He jumped in and drove away. He drove away very fast!

He soon found out that it is not good to drive <u>too</u> fast.

"What's your hurry?" asked a policeman.
"This isn't a racetrack, you know." He gave
Donald a ticket for driving too fast.

"I guess I should slow down," said Donald. As he drove along, he saw Huey, Dewey, and Louie. They were riding skateboards.

"Wait a minute, fellows. You are doing that all wrong!" Donald shouted. "Let me show you how to do it."

Well, Donald showed them, all right. He slipped. He fell. Donald found out that Huey, Dewey, and Louie were better on skateboards than he was.

As Goofy chugged along, he saw a hot-dog stand. Goofy's stomach began to growl. He was very hungry.

"I could eat ten hot dogs all by myself,"
he thought. "But Bessie and I just have to
keep moving. After all, we are in a race!" So
Goofy kept going. *Chug-a-chug-chug.*

By this time, Donald had given up riding a skateboard. But in a nearby park, a good ball game was going on.

"I think I'll stop," he said to himself. "A minute won't matter."

He watched the game for a while. The home team was way behind.

"They need me," said Donald. "And old Goofy is still nowhere in sight."

So Donald got into the game.
He thought he could hit the ball far. But
he could not hit the ball far that day.

Donald thought he could run fast. But he
could not run fast that day.
    Donald liked to be on the winning team.
But he was not on the winning team that day!

Meanwhile, Goofy chugged along. He was hot and thirsty. His throat was dry.

"Come on, Bessie," he said. "Slow and steady, steady and slow. That's the way we always go. We'll get something to drink later—after the race."

After the game, Donald was hot and thirsty, too. "I think I'll get a drink," he said. "A minute won't matter. I've still got plenty of time."

Goofy came to a high hill. Bessie huffed and puffed. She went very slowly.

"Come on, Bessie," he said. "Slow and steady, steady and slow. That's the way we always go. We can make it up this hill."

And Bessie's *chug—a—chug—chug, chug—a—chug—chug* sounded like "I will, I will."

At last Goofy and his car made it up that hill.

"Goofy's funny old car must have broken down! I haven't seen him for hours!" Donald laughed. "I might as well take my time. Old Goofy will never catch up!"

So Donald stopped for lunch. "A minute
won't matter," he said to himself.

Goofy was hungry too. But Goofy told Bessie, "We'll just keep going."

He went slowly, but he did not stop. He would not stop for anything.

After lunch, Donald raced down the road. He went faster than people on bikes. He went faster than people in trucks. He even went faster than people in other cars.

Donald tried to go faster than a train. But he could not. The people on the train smiled and waved at Donald. But the train went racing by.

Donald kept driving. But he did not drive for long. "Gee, I'm tired," he said. "I think I will take a nap. A minute won't matter."

So he drove off the road and stopped his car. He sat under a big, old tree. And Donald went right to sleep!

At last Goofy saw a sign that said Horner's Corners. He wondered if Donald was already there. He did not know.

"But we did our best," he said. "Slow
and steady, steady and slow. That's the way
we always go. Right, Bessie?"

Donald came to the sign that said Horner's Corners.

"Horner's Corners, here I come," he yelled. "Out of my way, everyone."

Va-ROOOOOM! The engine roared. The
tires squealed.

Donald stopped at Horner's Corners.
"This is some car," he said. "Poor Goofy!
I wonder when he'll get here."

Donald got out of his car. "Poor, poor
Goofy. He is sure going to feel bad. Well, I
will just tell him that he can't win them all.
I will even buy him an ice-cream cone!"
Donald went into the ice-cream shop.

To Donald's surprise, there sat Goofy!
"Why, hello there, Donald!" Goofy called.
"Where have you been?" He laughed. "I
guess I am not the slowpoke, after all."

"But—but—how could you win with
that funny old car?" asked Donald.
"Slow and steady," said Goofy. "Steady
and slow—that's the only way to go!"